WITHDRAWN

Dessert First

WITHDRAWN

Dessert First

by Hallie Durand
with illustrations
by Christine Davenier

atheneum books for young readers
NEW YORK   LONDON   TORONTO   SYDNEY

If you purchased this book without a cover, you should be aware that this book is stolen property. It was reported as "unsold and destroyed" to the publisher, and neither the author nor the publisher has received any payment for this "stripped book."

ATHENEUM BOOKS FOR YOUNG READERS
An imprint of Simon & Schuster Children's Publishing Division
1230 Avenue of the Americas, New York, New York 10020
This book is a work of fiction. Any references to historical events, real people, or real locales are used fictitiously. Other names, characters, places, and incidents are products of the author's imagination, and any resemblance to actual events or locales or persons, living or dead, is entirely coincidental.
Text copyright © 2009 by Hallie Durand
Illustrations copyright © 2009 by Christine Davenier
All rights reserved, including the right of reproduction in whole or in part in any form.
ATHENEUM BOOKS FOR YOUNG READERS is a registered trademark of Simon & Schuster, Inc.
For information about special discounts for bulk purchases, please contact Simon & Schuster Special Sales at 1-866-506-1949 or business@simonandschuster.com.
The Simon & Schuster Speakers Bureau can bring authors to your live event. For more information or to book an event, contact the Simon & Schuster Speakers Bureau at 1-866-248-3049 or visit our website at www.simonspeakers.com.
Also available in an Atheneum Books for Young Readers hardcover edition
Book design by Ann Bobco
The text for this book is set in Adobe Garamond Pro.
The illustrations for this book are rendered in pen and ink washes.
Manufactured in the United States of America

First Atheneum Books for Young Readers paperback edition May 2010
10 9 8 7 6 5 4 3 2
The Library of Congress has cataloged the hardcover edition as follows:
Durand, Hallie.
Dessert first / Hallie Durand ; illustrations by Christine Davenier.—1st ed.
p. cm.
Summary: Third-grader Dessert's love of treats leads to a change in her large family's dinner routine, then an awful mistake, and later a true sacrifice after her teacher, Mrs. Howdy Doody, urges students to march to the beat of their own drums.
ISBN: 978-1-4169-6385-1 (hc)
[1. Desserts—Fiction. 2. Schools—Fiction. 3. Restaurants—Fiction. 4. Family life—Fiction.] I. Davenier, Christine, ill. II. Title.
PZ7.D9313De 2009
[E]—dc22
2008011390
ISBN: 978-1-4169-6386-8 (pbk)
0410 OFF

*For Uptown Jenny Brown, who taught me how to share
my dessert and so much more. I love you.*

CHAPTER ONE

MRS. HOWDY DOODY

I don't know if Mrs. Howdy Doody is her real God-given name or not, but on the very first day of third grade, our teacher told us to call her that. She also told us, on that very first day, to march to our own drummers. Then she said, *"Watch and learn."* And right there in front of us, even though we didn't know her very well, she put on her white snowball slippers and marched around the classroom. She has big feet, and she took big steps, but she didn't make a sound because of the slippers.

"It's time to get acquainted," she said when she sat back down. I didn't know what to expect after the marching, but she reached under her desk and brought out a shiny piece of wood. She held it up for the class to see—it had a pair of roller skates and a pair of swim fins painted on it. "This is my coat of arms," she said, "and you can see that it tells you something about me. It tells you that I am a creature of land and sea, for starters.

"Now, reach into *your* desk," she said. I was disappointed that the "watching" part hadn't lasted very long, but I put my hand in my desk and pulled out a shiny piece of wood just like Mrs. Howdy Doody's. I reached in again and pulled out a perfectly new set of paints, with a brand-new brush for each color.

From what I could tell, Mrs. Howdy Doody and I were going to get along pretty well.

"You now have your raw materials," she said, as she held up her coat of arms again. "Traditionally," she continued, "a coat of arms is used to indicate your family distinctions. But I want yours to tell me what you are most passionate about.

"My dear happy learners," she said, "show me what you love!"

I'd never been called a happy learner before, and I wasn't sure I liked it, but I did try to think about what I loved. I saw that Donnie and Billy were already painting action figures. Donnie and Billy are twins, and I've known them for a long time. For sure, action figures are their passion. They always have a few in their pockets. Then Melissa R. asked if she could use rubber cement, and Emily V. asked for glitter. I didn't understand how they all knew what to do so fast.

Even *Amy D.* had something already. It was either a roller coaster or my sister Charlie's hair (they look the same the way she draws). I couldn't believe I was stuck in the same class as Amy D. again. We've been enemies since first grade, ever since she stuffed leaves in my mouth and called me "Tree."

It still makes me mad to think about that Leaf Stuffer, and here she was almost finished with her coat of arms when I hadn't even started.

What oh what did I love?

It certainly wasn't Charlie, and it certainly wasn't either of my brothers, Wolfgang or Mushy (they could be cute once in a while but not all the time). And it *certainly* was not mayonnaise. Just thinking about mayonnaise made me sick. There was only one thing I knew that I loved all the time. And that was my dog, Chunky—he's been with me since I was one. I wouldn't even need all the paints to color him; all I needed was black and white. I drew him to fill up the entire board because he is big—he's part

Rotty. I added a few gray hairs around his eyes, just to let people know how wise he is. Then I signed my name.

Dessert

You might want to know about the cherry. I call it flair. It could be on top of a banana split, a cornflake-cream-cheese cookie, a hot-fudge sundae, or even a freshly baked lemon square, like the ones Mummy made last night. Also, it shows my personal style.

Mrs. Howdy Doody came by and said, "That looks like a very large dog to me."

"This is Chunky," I said. "I've known him since I was one—that makes him forty-nine years old in our system."

"That's almost half a lifetime," Mrs. Howdy Doody said. Then she looked at my signature and said, "What in the wide world is that, Dessert Schneider?"

"It's a cherry," I said.

"A cherry?"

"Yes," I said. "A maraschino cherry."

"A maraschino cherry," said Mrs. Howdy Doody. "When it comes right down to it, that's really all you need in life, isn't it?"

"Plus something to put it on," I said, and we nodded at each other. I was convinced it was going to be an amazing year (except for Amy D.).

CHAPTER TWO

A FAMILY NIGHT

When I walked into our house after school the next day, I saw our big tub of crayons on the counter. This could mean only one thing—it was going to be another "family night" at Fondue Paris, our restaurant. I *love* fondue because it's cooked right at your table and you get to stick your food on the end of a skewer (it's like a mini back scratcher). After you stick your food on, you get to dip it in a big pot of melted cheese! But when we all go there together, something awful always happens. That's because Charlie, who's four, is going through a "phase," and Wolfgang and Mushy, who are two and one, are known as the Beasties. (That should tell you just about everything you need to know about them.)

Three hours later, just as I predicted, we were all sitting in our mini-van, on our way to Fondue. As soon as we walked through the revolving door, and I saw the Eiffel Tower in the middle of the room, I started wondering what today's flavor would be.

You've probably never seen a fondue tower. I hadn't either until Daddy and Mummy installed it in our restaurant four years ago. Mummy says it started as a simple way to honor her French heritage, and the idea was to have a small Eiffel Tower in the center of the restaurant. But my dad decided that *our*

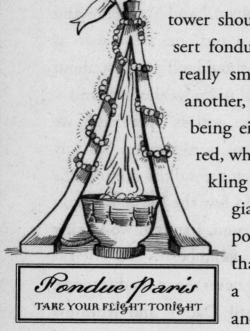

Fondue Paris
TAKE YOUR FLIGHT TONIGHT

tower should be full of dessert fondue (sometimes he's really smart). One way or another, the tower ended up being eight feet tall, with red, white, and blue twinkling lights. There's a giant silver fondue pot underneath it that's shaped like a witch's cauldron, and each day it's bubbling with a different flavor of sweet, delicious fondue. If you look closely, you can see the fondue go up the tube inside the tower, and once it reaches the top, it comes streaming back down through the middle. It's a beautiful thing to watch.

Then comes the fantastic part: You get to fill up your fondue bowl under the stream! The not-so-fantastic part is that somebody always seems to be watching to make sure you don't take too much or make a mess.

Guston came rushing over as soon as he saw us and he kissed me and everybody else on both cheeks (this took forever). Then he said, "Follow me." He led us to our table, Number Twelve, with only a mirror view of the fountain. Daddy always says, "There's not a bad seat in the house," because of the mirrors everywhere, but I think he's wrong. I've never been allowed to sit right next to the tower, but I am convinced it would be better than just watching that yummy fondue stream in a mirror.

After we sat down, the first thing I did was open my menu and take a look at the small sheet inside that told me today's special tower flavor. That little sheet told me it was Maisie's Melted Lollipop, which tastes like orange, lemon, and lime sherbet all mixed together. (It's one of the best we have.)

A few minutes later, Guston presented each of us with a pink ginger ale. At least that's what Charlie calls a Shirley Temple.

"You are now a third grader," Guston said to me, "so you will order first. Tell me what you like."

"Guess," I said.

He put his finger to his chin and said, "Of course it will be the coq au vin."

"Of course it won't," I said.

"Then I'm sure it will be the filet de boeuf," said Guston.

"Here's a clue," I said, and then I sang, "A-B-C-D-E—"

"F! F is for Fondue Flight!" Guston said.

"Yes!" I said.

"Your cheese?" he asked.

"My cheese better—"

"Be cheddar!" said Guston. "Of course it will be the cheddar!"

The Fondue Flight was the only thing we ever ordered, because you get to start with cheese fondue and you end up with a trip to the tower! (The "flight" is very popular.)

"How was Mrs. Howdy Doody today?" said Mummy.

"You wouldn't like her," I said.

"Why not?" said Mummy.

"Her socks," I said.

"What about her socks?"

"They don't match," I said.

"That's okay," said Mummy. "Sounds like she has her own fashion sense."

"Then how come it's not okay when mine don't match?"

"Well, she's your teacher," said Mummy, "and it's nice that she does things her own way. Did Billy and Donnie—"

"BILLY AND DONNIE!" Charlie shouted. "I'M GOING TO MARRY BILLY AND DONNIE!"

Guston appeared, ready to make our fondue. "Is there a wedding?" he asked.

"You'd better speak with Charlie about
that," I said.

"Voilà," he said, ignoring me, and he
placed one platter of bread cubes, apples,
carrots, potatoes, and pickles in between me
and Charlie and another between my parents.

"Ninety-seven flights last night!" Dad
said to Guston.

"They come for the tower," Guston replied
as he put a silver fondue pot on top of a skinny
metal frame, with the Sterno under it. He
smiled as he lit the can on fire. (I think the
Sterno looks like a can of tuna with blue Jell-O
in it.) There was a big flame for a second and
then it got smaller. Guston started cooking.

"The garlic," he said, as he threw it in and moved it all around the pot. Then he let me and Charlie dump in the cheese, and he added mustard and white wine. His arm moved like an egg beater, and he stirred fast for a long time.

"Dessert," he finally said, "you'll be my critic."

"Of course," I said. I took my skewer and put a big piece of bread on the end. Then I started rolling it in the fondue. When there was lots of cheese wrapped around my bread I took it out. I blew on it three times and put the whole thing in my mouth.

"It's heavenly," I said when I had finally swallowed it.

"Merci," he said.

Then Guston disappeared for a moment

and came back with a heap-
ing platter of french fries for
me and Charlie and the
Beasties—we like to dip
them in our fondue. (My
parents think it's gross.)

I took turns dipping pickles, then fries,
then pickles, then fries, and I didn't look up
till I was done.

"What else should we know about Mrs.
Howdy Doody?" said Mummy.

"Nothing. Can I go to the tower now?"
I said.

"*May* you go to the tower," said Mummy.

"*May* I go to the tower?" I said.

"You may," said Mummy, "and you may
take Charlie with you."

"I go too," said Wolfie, climbing down from his chair.

"You'll stay right here," said Mummy, putting him back in his seat.

Guston must have heard us, because there he was, taking our plates away. He always seems to be in the right place at the right time. A moment later he came back with a platter of strawberry hats, pretzel animals, and cookie braids.

I led Charlie over to the tower, and since nobody seemed to be watching I filled my bowl with the yummy melted orange-green-yellow fondue till it nearly overflowed. Then I kept guard for Charlie while she did the same thing. (I was hoping Mummy wouldn't notice. She does not like "excess.")

On our way back to Table Number Twelve, I saw in the mirrors that we wouldn't be staying much longer because Wolfie was

19

standing on his chair with a skewer in his hand. I watched Daddy trying to snatch it away and Mummy blocking Mushy's head. Then the chair toppled over, and Wolfie disappeared from view. By the time we got back, Daddy was dragging him out from under the table, and he said to us, "We'll be in the van."

And right then, Mushy started swiping the table like a windshield wiper. Mummy grabbed him and handed him to Daddy.

"Take him, too," she said.

Once it was quiet again, Charlie and Mummy and I took turns dipping. I dunked my cookie braid straight down and twirled until it looked like a rainbow totem pole. I put it into my mouth and let the whole thing turn into sugary soup. Next I skewered a strawberry hat and filled it with fondue. Then I dunked a pretzel animal, and it was salty and sweet at the same time.

"We can't forget about Dad," said Mummy. "Three more dips." I squeezed in another pretzel animal and two more totem poles and I felt good and comfortable. . . . even though I knew what was waiting for us in the van.

CHAPTER THREE

COURAGE AND DETERMINATION

On Monday I said, "Good morning, Mrs. Howdy Doody," and she said, "Good morning, Dessert."

"Who wants to march today?" Mrs. Howdy Doody asked, once we were all sitting at our desks. Most of us raised our hands.

"Amy D.," she said, "let me see you march!" Amy D. marched around the room. I did not enjoy watching her one bit, and even worse, she nudged my chair a little when she passed behind me.

Of course Mrs. Howdy Doody didn't notice—nobody ever noticed how mean

Amy D. was. Instead Mrs. Howdy Doody said, "I am inspired! In a perfect world, we'd all have the courage and determination to march to our own drummers. Think about that."

In a perfect world, I thought, *there wouldn't be an Amy D.*

That afternoon I had to do my homework like I always do. Mummy must have ESP, because the very second I finished, she appeared in the doorway and said it was time to clean my room. Now, my room is usually pretty bad, but today it was just horrible, and I realized that in a perfect world, Charlie would clean it for me. So I yelled, "Chaaaaaaaaarrrrrlieeeeeeeeeeeeeeeeeeee!" as loud as I could, and when she came into the dining room, I made a chewing noise in

23

her ear (that's our secret signal). See, she's old enough to help me out, but she's still kind of dumb. If I want her to do something, all I have to do is offer her some gum. (She's not supposed to have it till she's five.) Whenever I get a pack, I take a piece, and I break it into as many teeny bits as I can, and I store it in my jewelry box. Even though Charlie's in a "phase," she'll still clean my room for a tiny bit of gum. It's probably because she's dying to learn how to blow a bubble, and I don't think it's my job to tell her that it's never going to happen with a piece of gum smaller than a pea. She'll figure it out someday.

Anyway, as soon as she heard that noise, she followed me right up the stairs. "See this mess?" I said as we stood in my doorway.

"Clean it up." I made a chewing noise to make sure she got the message, and then I lay down on my bed to read while she worked.

"Is it cleaned enough?" she asked a little later.

I looked around and said, "In a perfect world, Charlie, you would empty that, too." I took my bookmark and pointed to my waste-basket. After she emptied it, I couldn't find anything else for her to do, so I said, "Charlie, you may get your gum."

Then Wolfie showed up singing "E-I-E-I-O," which means he's in a good mood. I was so glad my room was done that I let him and Charlie play with my teeny china dogs until I heard Daddy yelling, "Come and get it."

The three of us went down to the kitchen,

and Mummy and Mushy were already there, so Daddy put our meal on the table. I took one look at my plate and realized that in a perfect world, I would *not* be about to eat a turkey

burger, kettle chips, and baby carrots. In a perfect world, I would be about to eat a lemon square.

I didn't even feel like sitting down; instead I stood there and said, "Mummy and Daddy, in a perfect world, dessert comes before supper. My body is calling for dessert first."

"What are you talking about?" said Daddy.

I was still standing, and I cleared my throat and said, "Daddy. What I'm trying to say is that in a perfect world, lemon squares come before turkey burgers. I'm listening to my body."

"Well," said Mummy, "this isn't a perfect world. So you can tell your body that we don't eat dessert first in the Schneider household. Further, your turkey burger will get cold."

"Cold turkey burgers do not bother me," I said.

"You may not mind them," said Mummy, "but your father and I do. Turkey burgers are served warm."

"That's right," said Daddy. "You're from a food family. Nobody here is going to eat a cold T burger."

"Then my name must be 'Nobody' tonight," I said, full of courage and determination.

"What did you say?" Daddy asked. (The look on his face did not scare me.)

"I don't know," I continued, "but what I meant is that I'm marching to my own drummer. I'll heat up my burger in the microwave . . . *after* my lemon square." (I was not even nervous.)

"Dessert," said Daddy. "Sit down and eat."

"Mummy and Daddy," I said, "it's just that I DO NOT

LIKE eating supper before dessert anymore. That's how I feel."

"EAT YOUR BURGER," said Daddy. "NOW."

I could hear from his voice that I wasn't going to get my way tonight, and I wanted my lemon square. So I ate the burger, as slowly as possible, one bitty bite after another. Daddy was watching me but trying to look like he wasn't, and when I finished, he said, "Did you enjoy the burger?"

"I did," I said cheerfully, and I muttered "not" under my breath. I figured it was best to let Daddy think he'd won.

CHAPTER FOUR

PUT ONE FOOT
IN FRONT OF THE OTHER

At school the next morning, Mrs. Howdy Doody said, "Who would like to march?"

Emily V.'s hand went up fast, and Mrs. Howdy Doody said, "Emily V., take it away!"

Emily held her head so straight that she must have been practicing at home. She never did anything wrong.

When she finished, I raised my hand and said, "What if people don't want you to march to your own drummer, Mrs. Howdy Doody? What do you do then?"

"Put one foot in front of the other," she said.

"You mean keep marching?"

"Keep marching," she said. "Timing is everything."

"Okay," I said.

That evening we were having Mrs. Pepe's meat loaf, baked potatoes with sour cream and salt, and sweet green peas. (It seemed like Dad made meat loaf almost every week, and it seemed like he stuck more green things in it every week, too.) I put one foot in front of the other and said, "Mummy, leave the meat loaf in the oven because we're having dessert first tonight."

"Says who?" said Mummy.

"Says me," I answered bravely, as I

marched to the refrigerator to get out the rice pudding. "It would be such a shame for the meat loaf to get cold while we're eating dessert." (Rice pudding isn't my favorite dessert, especially not this time, because it had golden raisins instead of brown, but I still wanted it first.)

"There will be no pudding before supper in the Schneider household," Daddy said.

"And *why* will there be no pudding before supper in the Schneider household?" I asked. (I know I sounded fresh, but I couldn't stop myself.) "The meat loaf won't get cold because it's still in the oven."

"Close the refrigerator door," said Mummy.

"But it's just that my body is calling—"

"Stop talking," Daddy said. "And put the pudding away."

"No," I said, standing tall. "I'm marching to my own drummer."

"Get in your chair, Dessert," said Daddy. "You're eating meat loaf first, pudding last, *if* you get pudding at all. Consider that a warning."

I took one last look at the pudding, and stuck my finger in and licked it. Then I

pushed the plastic wrap down so nobody could tell. I went back to my chair and didn't say a word. I remembered what Mrs. Howdy Doody said: *Timing is everything.* Out came the meat loaf, and I kept my eyes on my plate and ate my slice, green things and all. I wished I could give some to Chunky, but Daddy was doing that pretending-not-to-watch-me thing.

CHAPTER FIVE

TIMING IS EVERYTHING

The very next afternoon, things weren't going well at home. I'll explain. I was doing my home-work upstairs because Charlie was pulling a wet towel all around the house and I didn't want to get blamed. I was nearly finished when I heard a very loud crash. And then I heard Wolfie's stool scraping across the kitchen floor.

Daddy was at Fondue, and I knew Mummy needed help, so I jumped out of my chair and two-stepped down the stairs.

The crash had come from the kitchen and that's where I found Mummy. She was on her knees cleaning up a whole bunch of broken dishes, while Mushy sat in a pile of sugar on the floor. Charlie was at the sink, and the water was running. Wolfie was stuffing the toaster with marshmallows.

First I unplugged the toaster so that Wolfie could not make "toast." Next I tried to turn off the water, but Charlie held her arms straight out to her sides and yelled, "I'M DOIN' DISHES!" So I grabbed her arm skin and pinched a little.

"OOOOOOOOOOOOOOOOOOW-WWWWWWW!" she screamed. "YOU'RE HURTING ME."

I pinched harder and said, "Turn the water—"

"OW OW OW OW OW OW OW OW

OW I'M HURT I'M HURT I'M HURT I'M HURT—"

I tipped her chair forward and she dropped to the floor. I grabbed her feet and started pulling. When Mushy saw this, he climbed on, and I dragged that whole screaming toboggan right into the living room. (I'm stronger than I look.)

I went back in with the vacuum and let Wolfie

suck up the sugar. He was pretty good at this because he rode it like a pony. I left the vacuum there for Mummy and I gave Wolfie some Tupperware (he loves to play with that stuff). It was pretty quiet again, so I went back upstairs to finish my work. And that's when I heard Mrs. Howdy Doody's voice in my head saying, *Timing is everything.* I started to think that tonight might be the night to get my dessert before supper.

So when I was done with my homework, I presented it to Mummy and said, "Madame, if you'll check this for me, I'll set the table for you."

"Sure," said Mummy. "Let me just see what Charlie and the Beasties are up to—they've been awfully quiet." So I set out all the big dinner plates with the little dessert plates on top. Then I went right into the cookie jar and took out five hermit cookies. I placed one in the center of each plate and stepped back to admire my work. It was so beautiful to see those cookies sitting right there on top. But when Mummy returned with Charlie and the Beasties and saw the table she said, "So that's why you offered to help."

"It's one of the reasons," I admitted, "but try the cookie first tonight, okay?" I buckled Mushy into his high chair while Charlie and Wolfie sat down, and we all waited to see what Mummy would do.

She looked around the table and finally said, "Very well then."

And after we each ate our hermit cookies (even Mummy), she served us our white-chicken chili and our corn cakes. I ate it all up, every single bit. Then I said, "Mummy, I have cleaned my plate."

Mummy looked over and said, "So you have." Then she noticed that Charlie, Wolfie, and even Mushy had cleaned their plates too, and she said, "This is a very pleasant surprise. Who knew?"

I guess I am the leader.

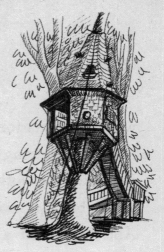

CHAPTER SIX

THE DOODY DRIVE

"Are you ready for the spirit assembly?" Mrs. Howdy Doody asked us one Tuesday morning a few weeks later. I hollered, "YES!" as loudly as I could, because the way I see it, if Mrs. Howdy Doody hadn't told me to march to my own drummer on that very first day of school, I wouldn't be eating dessert first every night. Mrs. Howdy Doody had changed my whole life.

"This month we are going to kick off Lambert Elementary School's First Annual Doody Drive," she said, "and we're going to find out what's possible when the whole school works together for a common goal. I see most of you are wearing red and white, as requested." I checked my clothes—I wasn't wearing much white, but I was wearing my favorite red dress. And I had on a pink undershirt, which I figured was both red *and* white.

Once we were all sitting down in the all-purpose room, Mr. Roberts, our principal, made an announcement.

"Good morning, compatriots," he said. "I'd like to dedicate this morning's spirit assembly to Mrs. Normana Howdy Doody. As many of you know, Mrs. Howdy Doody is celebrating her tenth year with Lambert Elementary this month, and in honor of that, I'd like to announce the FIRST ANNUAL DOODY DRIVE."

Mrs. Howdy Doody glided onstage in a dress that looked kind of like a gown.

"My dear happy learners," she practically sang. "Good morning!"

"GOOD MORNING!" we all shouted back.

"On my way to school today," she said, "I noticed that the leaves are turning just the teeniest bit golden. The golden leaves made me think about trees and the trees made me think about tree houses! Would you all like to play in a platform tree house during recess?"

"YESSSSSSSSSSSSSSSSSSSSSSSSSSSSS!" we all shouted.

"Then let the drive begin! Please welcome Donnie and Billy Blackett!"

I couldn't believe Donnie and Billy were up there! I hadn't heard anybody talk about this. They ran onto the stage, and each of them did a handspring. Their feet touched down at exactly the same time. I knew they were good at gymnastics, but I didn't know they could do handsprings. Then they marched together off the right side of the stage and returned a moment later with a gigantic poster. It said:

FIRST ANNUAL
DOODY DRIVE
BE A DOOZIE
MAKE A DIFFERENCE
ROUND UP YOUR
PLEDGES
&
TOGETHER WE'LL
BUILD A TREE HOUSE

Then Mrs. Howdy Doody said, clapping her hands, "EACH of you must be a doozie, my dear happy learners. EACH of you must be a champion! EACH of you must be extraordinary!

"Here's how it works: You each give up something you love. Your parents, in turn, make a pledge to you. And what this means is: one small sacrifice for you . . . one giant tree house for Lambert Elementary!"

Hmm. I wanted a tree house, but the part about giving something up sounded bad.

She held up the microphone again and said, "To kick things off, with you as my witnesses, I am going to make my promise to Principal Roberts.

"Principal Roberts, please come to center stage."

He stood by her side, and she announced, "Principal Roberts, I hereby pledge to give up peanut butter and jelly sandwiches."

"That will be a challenge," he said. "It's a worthy sacrifice, Mrs. Howdy Doody, and all for the greater good. I will pledge you two dollars a day."

"I will not let the school down, Principal Roberts," she said. They shook hands.

I couldn't believe Mrs. Howdy Doody was giving up peanut butter and jelly sandwiches! I had seen a jar of peanut butter in her top drawer, so I knew she loved it.

"Mrs. Howdy Doody," said Principal

Roberts, "*I* hereby pledge to give up watching ice hockey on TV."

"Surely that will not be easy for you," said Mrs. Howdy Doody. "It's a worthy sacrifice, and all for the greater good. I will pledge you two dollars a day." They shook hands.

Mrs. Howdy Doody looked out at us and said, "We've made our pledges. It's time for you to make yours. The contracts will be in your folders, and they are due back next Monday. TOGETHER WE'LL BUILD A TREE HOUSE!"

If only I could give up mayonnaise for my sacrifice. But my parents knew I hated it. I wasn't sure about this Doody Drive. I wasn't sure I wanted to make a worthy sacrifice.

CHAPTER SEVEN

BROWNIES BAKING

It didn't take long for me to forget about the Doody Drive, because when I came home from school, I smelled brownies baking. I marched straight into the family room and said to Mummy, "Is it my imagination, or do I smell brownies baking?"

"You smell more than brownies baking today, Dessert. You smell Double-Decker Chocolate Bars."

"Where are those Double-Decker Chocolate Bars, Mummy?"

"They're off-limits, Dessert."

"I could be your critic," I said.

"*Stay away from the Double-Ds,*" Mummy said.

"Crud," I said to myself, and since she was busy with Charlie, Wolfie, and Mushy, and Daddy was out of sight, I headed to the refrigerator. There was a white box on the bottom shelf, with a note on top that said: DO NOT TOUCH. THAT MEANS YOU. Crud. They were probably for a bake sale or something like that. But it wouldn't hurt to see what they looked like.

I took the lid off, and I nearly fainted. There, before my very eyes, was a full box of Double-Decker Chocolate Bars. I took a closer look and saw that there were actually twelve bars, sitting together neatly on Mummy's shiny turquoise paper. It seemed wrong that I'd only

had Double-Deckers three times in my life:
after I got two shots in my thigh when I was
four (and that shouldn't even count), when
Mummy made them for a cookie swap (the
one I got was barely visible), and at my sixth
birthday party (Mummy made them for the
parents, and I managed to "drop" one).

These must be for a bake sale. Charlie's
school was *always* having one. Mummy made

the best stuff for other people. And that just wasn't fair. It wasn't fair to her family. So I went ahead and picked one up. There was the thin, rich, brown fudge layer on the bottom. That layer was covered with a full half-inch of white frosting. On top of that was a dark-chocolate scribble.

I scraped the tiniest bit off the side and put it in my mouth. It was the chocolaty-est, vanilla-ee-est morsel ever. I nibbled along the edge a little more until . . . *plop*. What was that noise? I packed the box together as fast as I could and shut the fridge door. I edged my way out into the hall.

Phew. It was just the mail, with nothing for me, as usual. False alarm. But I promised myself that I would not go into that box again. Chunky saw me, and he put his head down and his eyes up. That means he wants to play, so I patted my leg, opened the front door, and started chasing him. It felt good to be out of the house. I'll probably never know if it's because Chunky's chubby or just kind-hearted, but I almost always catch him. (We make a good team.)

CHAPTER EIGHT

PRECAUTIONS

I woke up the next day with a smile on my face. I could tell it was cold out because there was frost on my windows, but knowing there were Double-Deckers in the fridge put me in a good mood. Just like every other morning, Wolfie started rattling his crib, which made Mushy start rattling *his* crib, which made Charlie wake up and start hollering "Mummy." I headed downstairs to get my breakfast. But first I wanted to make sure you couldn't tell I'd been in the box of Double-Ds.

I knew I could trust Chunky to stand up if anybody was coming (he's a good guard dog), so I opened the fridge door. The box was still there, and it still had that darn sign on it. Nobody was coming, so I took the lid off to check on them. I could see the tooth marks from yesterday. If I got caught, that would just be plain bad news, so I decided to smooth over the tooth marks a little. The more I smoothed it, the worse it looked. Whoever saw it would know it was picked at, so I was going to have to eat it. It was only one bar. There would still be eleven left. I stuck it in my mouth and oh! It was like eating a gooey-hard-vanilla-chocolate-cookie-cake for breakfast. It was wondrous. I shifted the box around a little, and it still looked full, so I felt pretty much okay.

As a precautionary measure, I put two slices of bread in the toaster. My parents would be *so* glad that I was making my own breakfast. They would never know what I'd done. And as Daddy always says, I'm from a food family. It was only natural to want to sample the Double-Ds. I spread the toast with peanut butter and butter and fed it to the Chunkamonka (he *loves* peanut butter).

I was full of goodwill, so I zipped up the stairs, put on some clothes, and said to Mummy and Daddy, "I'm dressed and I'm fed and my backpack is ready and I have fifteen minutes left. What can I do?"

"Just in time," replied Mummy. "Would you help Charlie choose her outfit? It sounds like she's having trouble."

"Piece o' cake," I said, even though I don't like helping her get dressed one bit. If her socks don't cover her toes exactly evenly, she starts whining, and then when I try to fix them she kicks me. But I was feeling so good and so chocolaty that I hummed "Oh, What a Beautiful Morning" as I walked into her room.

CHAPTER NINE

AFTER SCHOOL

That afternoon, when I got home from school, our babysitter Pam was there. I was confused because Mummy's usually home on Wednesdays.

Pam saw the look on my face and said, "When the thermometer drops—"

"Order more cheese," I finished. That explained it. On the first cold day of each year, Mummy and Daddy are always short-staffed—Mummy says it's because fondue is a "comfort food," so when the weather is chilly, everybody wants it.

Pam was always curious about what I was learning at school, so I let her empty my backpack for me.

"Dessert, this looks like a perfect spelling test," she said.

"It is," I said.

"And a minus two on your math homework?"

"Uh-huh," I said.

"Let's see what you got wrong," she said. "Dessert, you left two blanks!"

"Yeah," I said. "I know. I was trying to think of a worthy sacrifice."

"A what?"

"For the Doody Drive," I said. "I'm supposed to give up something I love so we can build a tree house."

"Isn't your teacher's name Doody?"

"Yup," I said, "and this is her idea." I pulled the crumpled contract out of the front of my backpack and handed it to Pam.

The phone rang.

"One hundred?" said Pam.

"Got it!"

"Cool."

Mummy and Daddy already had a hundred covers at Fondue. One hundred hungry people were already there. They needed more Sterno, lots more cans of Sterno. So Pam put me in charge of Charlie and left for Fondue with the boxes of Sterno and the Beasties. I figured I had no more than ten minutes, so I got right to work.

I put the Doody contract on the dining-room table and made the chewing noise to Charlie. "Time for school," I said. I led the way up to my room, pointed at the bed, and said, "Take a nap." Thank goodness for my gum supply. I could get her to do practically

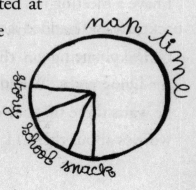

anything for the teensiest piece. I pulled back the comforter, and she lay right down, still as a soldier. "Good work," I said. "I'll be right back. I have a meeting in the faculty room."

I went back downstairs and there was Chunky, sitting on the big window seat in the living room. Whenever the Beasties leave, he waits there till they come back. (I think he worries about them.) I *had* to look at that box again, just to make sure it had really shifted okay. I opened the fridge, took off the lid, and once more, I admired the Double-Ds. I was enchanted with those bars—the swirly chocolate on top seemed even shinier than it had that morning. They were hard to resist. And Pam hadn't offered me an after-school snack, so I was on my own today. If I just cut off a little strip, no one would be able to tell I'd eaten any. I got a steak knife and cut a little piece off the side of one of the bars, a very thin slice. The bar looked just a tiny bit smaller. And that little strip was so tasty. I studied the bars in the box, and the one that was smaller seemed to stick out. I was worried about that one bar looking skinnier, so I sat right down and "shaved" each bar just the smallest bit. Those thin strips were the best snack I had ever had, and it was good to see that the bars were all the same size now. The box still looked pretty much untouched. Nobody would ever know. I put it back on the shelf and closed the refrigerator door.

I washed the knife, put it away, and checked in the mirror to make sure there was no chocolate on my mouth. There wasn't, so I ran back upstairs and said to Charlie, "Wake up! Time to read." And just like that, Charlie sat straight up. I gave her a tiny bit of gum. "Watch and learn," I said, as I opened my book.

"Fondue's jumpin'!" Pam yelled up when she got home. "How are you guys?"

"Good," I called back.

"Come down here!" said Pam. "I want to hear more about that Doody thing."

Shoot. I'd forgotten all about it again. What *was* I going to give up, anyway? At least I had five more days before I needed to hand that contract in.

CHAPTER TEN

A MIDNIGHT SNACK

Chunky sleeps on my bed. He weighs 140 pounds, but I always tell him he is light as a feather because he has a great spirit. It's my job to take him out before I go to bed at nine o'clock, and it's my job to let him out again in the morning when the bus comes.

So that evening I got ready for bed, and I let Chunky out and in, and we said good night. But at exactly 12:32 a.m., I woke up. Chunky was hopping around my room like there were thumbtacks on the floor. I took him straight downstairs, and on the way to

the back door, I passed the refrigerator. And I remembered something. I remembered that those Double-Deckers were in there.

I opened the door for Chunky, and he trotted out. I looked over at the fridge. It was almost like it was calling my name. I was sure I heard it whispering, "Deeessseeerrrttt." Chunky came back inside, and I shut the door. Then I saw *him* look at the fridge. He must have heard the same thing I did. I connected eyes with him. "Do you want a midnight snack?" I said.

I guess he did, because he stood in the doorway like a crossing guard. I opened the fridge and set down a big piece of smoked ham for Chunky. With a *whoosh* his tongue swept up the ham. And then I saw before me the box of Double-Ds. My arms tingled just looking at them. I had only had one taco for supper, and if ever there was a night for a midnight snack, this was it. On top of that, it wasn't right that these delicious bars would be wasted at a bake sale. The sign was still there, and all it did was remind me of all the times Mummy baked stuff that I didn't get to eat. But what if I got caught? Mummy and Daddy would kill me.

The next thing I saw was that my hand opened the box and touched the top of one of the bars. It was smooth and silky. My hand felt the sides and inched its way across the top, and my hand raised the bar out of the box and all the way into my mouth. My mouth chewed the bar, and then my hand went back and raised another out of the box. That bar went into my mouth too, and I watched as my hand went back and raised another bar and put it into my mouth. My hand was on automatic. It kept reaching in and raising one

bar after another after another. It kept putting one bar after another after another into
my mouth. My mouth kept chewing them,
and my hand kept taking them.

My hand emptied the box. My hand
pushed the box back into the fridge, and my
body went back up to bed.

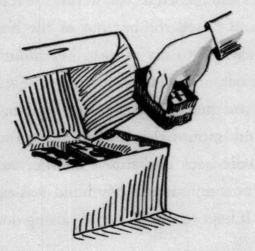

CHAPTER ELEVEN

I DON'T FEEL GOOD

I was awake before the sun came up, because I didn't feel very good. Something felt very wrong. Did I have a bad dream, or did I really eat all the Double-Decker Bars? There *was* a big brown circle of drool on my pillow. The circle smelled like chocolate. Chunky licked my face, and he smelled like ham. And then I saw my fingers. They were covered with sticky brown and white stuff. I smelled it. The sticky brown and white stuff smelled like Double-Decker Chocolate Bars.

I prayed that what I thought might have happened hadn't happened. I prayed that it wasn't true. I ran downstairs. I opened the fridge. Oh, crud. The lid was not on the box the right way. I opened it up. There was nothing inside but the turquoise paper. I had to sit down. What oh what had I done? Then I remembered my hand. I remembered my hand raising bars out of the box. I remembered my hand putting bars in my mouth. I remembered my mouth chewing the bars. That's why I didn't feel good.

I could *not* get caught. I needed a plan. I needed a plan before Mummy woke up. And then Chunky put out a paw—I think he wanted to remind me that we were in this together. But I knew I was in it alone. If only chocolate were death for humans instead of dogs, I would be dead by now. If I were dead by now, I wouldn't need a plan. But I was alive, and I didn't have much time.

I was pretty sure the Double-Ds were for a bake sale. That must have been why Mummy put the sign on the box. I had to believe it. Because if I didn't believe it, I would not have any hope. The sun was coming up. Time was not on my side. Mummy would be downstairs soon. Holy holy crud. For sure, this was the worst thing I had ever done. If I got caught, the punishment would be the worst punishment ever.

Okay. I had to get rid of Mummy's telltale turquoise paper (she uses it for everything). I was afraid whoever bought the Double-Ds would recognize Mummy's turquoise paper when they opened the box. I crumpled it into a little ball and hid it in the bottom of the garbage. But what could I refill the box with? What did I have that weighed the same as twelve Double-Decker Chocolate Bars?

The sun was getting brighter. I took the empty box downstairs to see what we had in the supply closet. Right next to the boxes of Sterno was a case of guest checks. I held one pad in my hand, and it seemed to be the right size and weight, so I started laying them side by side, four across and two down.

I put the lid back and it felt just about right, as best I could remember. My heart was beating pretty badly, the sun was almost up, and I thought I might have a stroke. My hands were shaking as I put the lid back on, with the note still attached. It was a relief to see that it pretty much looked like it did before, but I was nervous. I tucked the box right back in the fridge where I'd found it, and I convinced myself that whoever bought the Double-Ds would not be able to trace it to us. The guest checks didn't say "Fondue Paris" or anything like that.

Then I heard footsteps on the second floor, right above my head. I prayed for help. I sucked in my breath and waited. Then I heard a toilet flush. More footsteps. Then nothing. Whew. I crawled up the stairs and back into my room. My heart was pumping fast, but I managed to get some clothes on. Then I waited in my room until 7:10 a.m., my usual wake-up time.

I felt terrible in my stomach, and I had sweat all over, but I didn't want anybody to know. Like I normally would, I went downstairs to get my breakfast, even though I wasn't hungry.

Mummy walked in the kitchen right after me, dressed and ready to go. And Charlie came right behind her. Daddy was still sleeping.

"Hello, Dessert!" she said.

"Where are you going today, Mummy?" I asked, hoping she would mention the bake sale.

"To Charlie's school," she said. "I'm the helping parent today."

"Anything special goin' on?" I said, trying not to let my voice shake. "Like a bake sale or anything like that?" (I wanted to sound casual.)

"Not that I know of," said Mummy, "but I'm bringing rice for the sensory table."

"H-huh? I thought I saw a note that there was some kind of bake sale today," I lied.

"Nope, no sale at all, Dessert. What makes you so interested in bake sales, anyway?"

I felt like I was going to die. *The Double-Ds had not been made for a bake sale.* My voice came out a little higher than usual when I said, "Oh, you know, the Doody Drive got me thinking about raising money." (Mummy didn't notice my voice.)

"We'll have to talk about that, honey. I saw that paper on the dining table."

"Yeh," I said. I smiled at her, but it wasn't a real smile.

"Hi, Pam," said Mummy when Pam came through the door a second later. "Wolfgang and Mushy are just about ready for breakfast, and Charlie and I should be home around lunchtime. Please make sure Dessert catches the bus, and if you have a chance, run these plates through the rinse cycle. We're doing something special tonight."

"Something special?" I said (my voice was still high).

"Yes, Dessert, something very special. I'll see you after school." Mummy blew me a kiss and left with Charlie.

When I arrived at school, I mumbled, "Good morning, Mrs. Howdy Doody."

"Good morning, Dessert! Ask me why I am doing especially well today."

"Okay," I said. (It didn't seem like I had a choice.) "Why?"

"Today is Wednesday!" she said. "Wednesdays are one of my favorite days of the week, because you never know what you might learn by Friday." Then she rang her bell.

"My dear happy learners," she said to the whole class, "on my way to school this morning, I thought to myself, if we all work together, soon we'll have a tree house. And the view from that tree house is going to be all the

more glorious because we are making sacrifices to build it. So tell me, how many of you have decided what you are going to give up?" Everybody but me raised their hands.

"Just as I thought," she said. "You are an exceptional class! I'd like you all to write down what you're giving up on slips of paper, and if

you haven't decided yet, you can write down your possibilities." Then she put on her snowball slippers and marched around the classroom, handing out the colored slips of paper. Usually I liked her slippers, but not today.

When all twenty-one of us had handed in our slips, Mrs. Howdy Doody read them out loud.

"Makeup." (Geezy Lou)

"Tater tots." (Evan C.)

"It's a surprise!" (Amy D.)

"Action figures." (Billy B.)

"Action figures." (Donnie B.)

"Hot dogs." (Tammy S.)

"Chips." (Jeanne S.)

"Computer games." (Charlotte R.)

"Stickers." (Sam C.)

"Making knots." (Sharon S.)

"Scissors." (Jack S.)

"Remote-control trucks." (Marshall W.)

"Now and Laters." (Bonnie A.)

"Gumballs." (Emily V.)

"Racing my guinea pig." (Pat D.)

"Eating in the family room." (Grace E.)

"Batteries." (Lois Z.)

"Barbies." (Melissa R.)

"Mean faces." (Michael A.)

"Leaving my shoes out." (Josh M.)

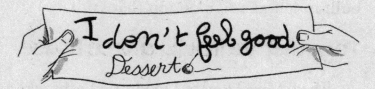

When Mrs. Howdy Doody got to my slip, she said, "Dessert, I didn't know you were under the weather. Do you need to go see Nurse Thomas?"

"No."

"We'll speak in a moment, Dessert, but for now, I'd like you all to close your eyes until I say 'tree house.'"

I closed my eyes and it sounded like Mrs. Howdy Doody was rearranging the furniture. Several minutes later, she said, "Tree house!" and we opened our eyes, and there before us was a big tree with a tree house built in it and a sign on top that said:

Together we'll build a tree house

Then Mrs. Howdy Doody tied a brown ribbon through each slip (except for mine) and hung them up.

Looking at that tree, with everybody being so darned jolly, made me burst into tears.

Mrs. Howdy Doody came over to my desk, handed me my slip, and said, "Why don't you feel good?"

The cries got worse, and I couldn't catch my breath. I put my head on my desk. Mrs. Howdy Doody whispered, "Do you want to talk?"

I managed to get a breath and I said, "Mrs. Howdy Doody, I am going to get caught."

"You're going to get caught?"

"Remember Chunky?"

"How could I forget Chunky!" she said.

"We had a midnight snack last night, and I ate every one of the Double-Decker Chocolate Bars Mummy had in the fridge, even though I wasn't supposed to. And that's not all."

"What else went wrong, Dessert?"

"I covered it up."

"Okay," she said, "first things first. Do your parents know that you ate the Double-Deckers?"

"Not yet."

"Are you sorry?"

"Yes."

Do you want to say you're sorry but you don't know how?"

"Sort of."

"I can help you," Mrs. Howdy Doody said. "Because I know how you feel. And sometimes it helps when you know that someone else understands how you feel. Come. We'll speak in the tulip garden."

CHAPTER TWELVE

CAN MAN

Mrs. Howdy Doody led me into the tulip garden, and we sat on a little wooden bench.

"When I was a little girl," she said, "one of my jobs was 'can man.' We lived on a farm in the snowbelt region of the Northeast, and my job was to take all the recycling out to the barn every night, since we didn't have enough room to store it in our kitchen. Now, the

barn was quite a distance from the house, and sometimes I forgot about my responsibility until it was dark. But I knew very well that if the cans and bottles were still in the kitchen when my father woke up, I would be in the doghouse. Well, I wouldn't *literally* be in a doghouse, Dessert, but my father would not be pleased with me.

"So, winter came, and with it a great deal of snow. The trip to the barn was harder and the air was colder. Are you following me?"

"Yes," I said.

"Okay," she said. "Now, I was old enough to know that when it was snowing in the evening in the snowbelt region, it would probably continue to snow until morning. So, on those kind of nights, I dropped the cans and bottles as soon as I started walking, *knowing* they would be covered in white by morning, *confident* that I would not be caught. Is this a familiar feeling to you?"

"Sort of," I said.

"I thought it might be," said Mrs. Howdy Doody, "because I was just about your age when this happened to me. Spring came as

it always does, Dessert, and the snow melted. Our lawn was littered with cans and bottles. To my surprise, my father did not yell at me. Instead, he helped me pick them up. Together we loaded them into the back of our pickup and took them to the scrap yard. Together we unloaded them, and in exchange, we received five dollars and seventy-five cents.

"'Normana,' said my father, as he counted each bill and put them in his wallet. 'I wanted *you* to have this money, but you deceived me.'

"I will never forget the way I felt as he closed his wallet and put it back in his pants. And I will never forget the way those coins sounded, jingling around in his front pocket.

"What it boils down to is this, Dessert: If you deceive your parents, there is a chance you will be caught. It's usually best to consider the repercussions before taking action. But for today, you should probably look your parents straight in the eye when you get home, and you should probably start talking. It'll be okay. I sit here beside you today as proof.

"Now let's get to work!"

I still felt small, but I was a tiny bit relieved that somebody else, especially my teacher, had been almost as bad as I had been.

Every time I looked at the clock, it was a little closer to 2:35. I was gathering my courage to make my confession when I got home. But as it turned out I didn't have a chance, because when I walked in the door, Daddy said, "Your mum is taking a nap with the

Beasties, Dessert. Can you help me make the quiche Lorraine?"

Darn it. Usually I would say "Piece o' cake," because I love helping with quiche Lorraine, especially the eating part—it's so buttery and bubbly and cheesy. But today I had my confession on my mind, so I didn't say a word. The weird thing is that Daddy just handed me the rolling pin. And that's when I understood that sometimes people think you are saying something when you aren't. I silently rolled out the dough and put it in the giant pie pan and fluted the edges (I could practically flute with my eyes closed, and I usually like to because it makes the edges of the pie look pretty). When I finished, I managed to say in a teeny voice, "I'm going upstairs."

"Okay, Dessert."

I lay on my bed with Chunky, thinking about the Double-Deckers. Mummy was bound to wake up soon, which meant I had to get up my courage so I could tell my parents. Chunky put his head on my belly and began to close his eyes.

"How am I going to get up my courage?" I whispered to him.

His big, black, sad eyes told me how sorry he was.

I stroked his head and whispered, "I know you are."

And when I said that, Chunky moved a little closer to me and put his nose on my neck. Then I knew for sure that he would take the blame for me if he could, because that's the kind of dog he is. (I really love him.)

CHAPTER THIRTEEN

AAAAHHHHHHHHHHH!

I'm not sure how long we lay there, but the feeling of friendship brought back some of my courage, so I decided that the time had come to make the confession. I tiptoed downstairs and approached the kitchen. But the second Mummy heard me, she said, "Dessert, could you help the Beasties wash their hands? It's time for our celebration!"

I felt a huge lump in my throat. I couldn't say a word. But Mummy didn't notice.

Once we all got settled at the table, I didn't have a chance to speak because

Mummy asked us to listen. She said, "Tonight my mother would have turned seventy-five. How I wish she were here with us." Then she paused for a moment. She started again and said, "Her favorite treat was a recipe of unknown origin. She found it, all typed up in English, in the overhead baggage compartment on a plane trip from Paris to New York. That flight was the last one she took." Mummy's voice got bumpy. "Your grandmother waved that recipe around and asked if it belonged to anyone. I'll never be sure if it was because she asked in French or because it was fate, but nobody claimed it." Now Mummy was smiling a little bit. "So she placed the card in her wallet and accepted it as her own." And then Mummy folded her hands across her plate and looked at all of us. "Even though she left us before her time, tonight we will honor her by sharing her favorite dessert." Her voice got a little quieter and she said, "We will enjoy it as if she were here at the table with us."

My face was hot. I said, "Mummy, there is something I need to tell you." (My voice was shaky, but it was back.)

"Dessert, tell me after our treat. Would you go get the white box out of the refrigerator?"

"The white box with the note on it?"

"Yes, honey, I'm glad you saw the note. I hope your father did too."

"Mummy, I have—"

"HAPPY BIRTHDAY TO GRANDMA, HAPPY BIRTHDAY TO—"

"Charlie," said Mummy, "let's wait till Dessert gets the box."

"But . . . Grandma's not here," I said.

"Oh, Dessert, bring out that box. We are celebrating her life tonight!"

I didn't move.

Mummy finally looked at me. "What's wrong, Dessert?" she asked.

"I don't feel very good," was all I could get out.

"You'll feel better in a minute," said Mummy, and she stood up, went right to the refrigerator, and came back with the white box. She set it down on the table and took off the lid. She gasped.

Daddy saw the guest checks. "WHAT—"

"AHHHHHHHHHHHHHHH-HHHHHHHHHHHHHHHHHH-

H H H H H H H H H H H H H H H H !"
I screamed. The cork had popped out of me.
"AHHHHHHHHHHHHHHH!
AHHHHHHHHHHHAAAA-
AAAAAAHHHHHHHHHHHH-
HHHHHHHHHHHHHHHH,"
I kept screaming as I ran upstairs, with
Chunky right behind me. "AAAAAAA-
A A A A A A A H H H H H H -
H H H H H H H H H H H H H
A A A A A A A A A A A A A A A A
HHHHHHHHHHHHHHHHH-
HHHH!" My head was gonna blow up.
Daddy came charging up behind me with the
box in his hand. When he got to my room, he
dumped the guest checks on the floor. "What
were you thinking?" he said.

AAAAHHHHHHHHHHH!

"AAAAAHHHHHHH-HHHHHHHHHHHHHHH AAAHHHHHHHHHHHH-HHHHHHHHHHHHH!"

I kept screaming. Then Mummy came in, followed by Charlie and Wolfgang. A few moments later, Mushy appeared. Mummy looked like a dragon. Her mouth opened.

"AHHHHHHHH- HHHHHHHHHHH AAHHHHHHHHHHH- HHHHHHHHHHHHH- HHHH!"

And then she stopped.

And the silence was worse than the screams. I said a prayer to the rug. Then Mummy said flatly, "Find a way to show us you're sorry." She turned to leave the room, looked back at me, and said, "You can study your carpet until you figure out how."

She and Daddy walked out, and so did Charlie and Mushy. Wolfie was the last to leave, and as he did he said, "Sowwy," with a scared smile on his face. It made me feel worse.

I looked at my ceiling and said, "I'm sorry, Grandma, I'm sorry," and I meant it. Why oh why hadn't I stayed away from the Double-Ds like the note said? I had been caught. And not only that, the feeling I was having was a terrible one. It was like being sick and embarrassed and afraid at the same time, with nowhere to go.

What could I ever do to show I was sorry? I went down under my comforter, and Chunky was at my side. At least he still liked me. I knew nobody else in our house did.

CHAPTER FOURTEEN

I'M SORRY

I'm sure you know that I did not wake up
full of glory. But I *was* a little hungry. I was
hungry because I had missed my quiche
Lorraine. I squiched my way downstairs. I
made a little bowl of Rice Krispies and ate
quietly. I got dressed, and then I slinked
back into bed. Right before it was time for
the bus, I squiched back downstairs, grabbed
my backpack, let Chunky out, and waited in
front of the house.

When I saw Mrs. Howdy Doody at
school, I didn't say anything.

But she said, "Hello, Dessert. Are you present or absent?"

"Mrs. Howdy Doody," I said, "how am I going to show I'm sorry?"

"You're going to do it with your own style, Dessert," she said. "Try to think like you usually do."

"Think like I usually do?" I asked. "That's how I got into trouble."

"And that's how you'll get out of trouble too," she said.

I didn't want to talk to Mrs. Howdy Doody anymore today. What did she mean, think like I usually do? If I was thinking in the first place, how could I *not* be thinking like I usually do?

When the bus dropped me off that

afternoon, I walked in the door and saw Mummy and Daddy sitting on the stairs. I took a deep breath and kept my head down. I couldn't stand to look at my parents.

"I'm going up to study my carpet," I said as I passed between them. "I didn't consider the repercussions before taking action."

"Pardon?" said Mummy.

"Nothing," I said as I went into my room and shut the door.

I knew I needed to talk to somebody, and there was Chunky, sitting on my bed, as if he'd been expecting me all day. "How am I supposed to think like I usually do?" I said to him. He came over to me, so I rubbed him on the ears. We sat down there on my floor, and I said, "What are we going to do?"

Then I heard something thudding against my door, and Chunky's ears perked up, so I went over and opened it. There stood Wolfie, with Mushy at his side. All they had on were their diapers.

Mushy burped and Wolfie said, "You a pig," and they both started laughing. Then Mushy burped again and Wolfie said louder, "YOU A PIG!" and they came in. Mushy burped again, but then Mummy appeared and scooped them up and touched my hair and said, "You okay?"

"No."

"Got any ideas yet?"

"No."

"Let me know if you want to talk, 'kay?"

"'Kay."

I don't know if it's because I was think-ing like I usually do or because Wolfie said "Pig," but right there and then I had the answer. If Mushy was a pig, then I was definitely a hog, because only a hog would eat all of the Double-Ds—how could I have taken them from my own grandmother? The same grandmother who had given me my name. Mummy told me that when I was born, Grandma Reine said, *"Mon dessert est servi,"* which means "My dessert is served," but in French it sounds like *day-zair*. So even though my real God-given name is Donahue Penelope Schneider, I have always been called Dessert.

I had to make it up to Grandma Reine— I had to give her back the Double-Ds, and there was only one way to do it. I was going to have to talk to Dominique, the pastry chef, which meant I would have to try to catch her in a good mood. (I was a little afraid of her.) Not only that, but I was going to have to find a way to get to Fondue when she was there. I knew that she did most of her baking on Saturdays, so maybe I could offer to work. But I was also going to need a copy of the Double-Decker Chocolate Bar recipe.

I found Mummy downstairs and said, "May I have Grandma's Double-Decker Chocolate Bar recipe?"

I think she wanted to help me, because she gave it to me right away, without asking any questions. I went up to Dad's office and copied it, and then I snuck back downstairs and stuck a note on the oven door.

I didn't sign my name, because I was the only kid in the house who could write. They'd know who I was.

Dear Mummy
and Daddy,
I think I know
how to show I
am sorry. Please
come upstairs
when you are
ready to hear it.

CHAPTER FIFTEEN

THE PROPOSAL

I waited in my room, sitting a bit taller because I had a plan. About half an hour later, my parents came in. I still didn't want to look at them, so I kept my eyes down as I said, "Mummy and Daddy, I know how to show I'm sorry."

"Go on," said Mummy.

"May I work at Fondue on Saturday?"

"Work at Fondue?" asked Mummy. "Is that how you're going to show you're sorry?"

"It's part of my plan," I said, looking up at her. (I could see her eyes begin to crinkle.)

Daddy cleared his throat. "Like I often say, Dessert, you're from a food family," he said. "There's always enough side work at Fondue, that's one thing I know. The mayor's coming for a luncheon Saturday, so we're working brunch. There's a birthday party, too; you can help Guston with that."

Mummy's eyes were really crinkling now and her whole face began smiling. "We're glad you have a plan," she said.

CHAPTER SIXTEEN

A BIRTHDAY SURPRISE

As soon as we got to Fondue on Saturday, Daddy took me to Guston. The birthday party was scheduled for eleven thirty, and I would go home with Mummy and Daddy after cleanup. All I really wanted was to get Dominique to bake the Double-Ds, but I didn't want my parents to know that—I wanted it to be a surprise.

"Bonjour, ma chérie," said Guston. "I hope you like birthday parties, because today we have one for twelve fourth graders. Let's see what fondues they request. Malted Milk Ball,

Saltwater Taffy, Nuts for Nutella, and Maple Butter Ribbon."

I couldn't believe it. Maple Butter Ribbon was one of the few fondues I'd never tasted. Maybe I'd get to try it.

"Take this to Dominique," said Guston, "and tell her the children will be here in less than forty-five minutes."

Oh, how I hoped she was in a good mood. I started on my way to the pastry station, looking at the list. Did it really say "Dolan" at the top? D-O-L-A-N. It did. I prayed that it was spelled wrong, because that was Amy's last name. But Amy wasn't in fourth grade. It couldn't be the Leaf Stuffer. But what if she had a sister or brother? I handed the list to Dominique.

"Let's see what the kiddies are having today," she said. "Four party fondues."

In a second Dominique had all the flames going high, and she was beginning to stir like mad. With that scarf around her head, she looked scary. "Don't just stand there, Dessert, get yourself an apron!"

"Where's—"

"On the hook. Right over there." I scurried away. (I was afraid this was not a good-mood day.)

"My corn syrup! WHERE'S MY CORN SYRUP?"

Guston appeared, like magic, and said, "Here is your corn syrup."

I put on my apron, and Guston said, "Dessert, you are going to be a runner today. That means you run around and do what I tell you. First you will pass out the berets when the guests arrive." He went into the dining room and was back in no time. "*Zut!* They are early! I will finish preparing the table. Go to the door and stall them with the berets."

I took the box of berets and walked toward the door. And that's when I saw Amy D.

She saw me, too.

"What are *you* doing here?" she asked. "It's *my* sister's birthday."

"I know," I lied.

"If you're our server—"

"Shhh," I said.

"Don't shush me, Dessert."

"Listen, Amy. I'm only working—"

"*You're working?!* Wait till I tell my sister," Amy said. "Hey, Julie, Dessert's our waiter today. This is going to be the best party *ever*! Take my coat, Dessert."

I ignored her and started handing out the berets. I gave each of the older girls a pretty blue beret with a tiny French flag embroidered on the front. Then I looked at Amy and said, "Looks like you get pink, Amy. It's *such* a pretty color." (I knew she *hated* pink.)

"I'm not wearing that, Dessert. Give me a blue one."

"I'm sorry, but I ran out of blue." Then I crossed my arms and said, "No beret, no fondue. Rules are rules."

She hissed at me. I turned away and noticed that Guston was motioning us to come to the table. When I reached him, he said, "Smooth service, Dessert. *Merci*." (Little did he know.)

"Piece o' cake," I said.

"See how Dom is coming along now."

I took a walk back to her station, and she had all the fondues bubbling on the stove.

"How does a pastry chef end up making kiddy fondue?" she said.

"This is a beautiful cake," I said, as I studied the birthday cake she had baked. "What kind is it?"

"Nine-egg pound cake," she said. "Why?"

"'Cause your cakes are always the best." (I was hoping she liked compliments.)

"The best?" she said. "You really think so?"

"The *best*," I said.

"Well, it's just going to get sliced for fondue," she said.

"But I bet it tastes wonderful," I said. "I'm sorry it's going to Amy's sister."

"No time for sorry," she said. "Take this

out to the party. By the time they finish singing, the fondue will be ready." She did not wait for a reply before she put the huge cake, on its huge platter, in my arms. The cake was almost touching my mouth. I didn't lick it, though. I walked it right out to Guston and put it in his hands as fast as I could.

Amy D. was sitting at the far end of the table when the "Happy Birthday" song began. I sang along under my breath.

"Oh my dear friend Amy D.,
Yoo-hoo look so u-u-glee,
In that horrible pink beraaaaayyyyyyyy,
That I made you wear today."

Her sister blew out the candles, and Guston began cutting the beautiful cake into fondue-sized squares. Dominique was right about that. When all the plates were ready, Guston said, "Dessert, please serve our guests."

I started at the head of the table, knowing that Amy D. was on the other end. When I reached her, she said, "This table is rocking, Dessert." She looked me in the eye and said, "Fix it." Guston was watching, so I had to put on a fake smile.

"In a minute," I said pleasantly, even though I wanted to do something bad. I set down the last plate of cake and brought over a menu to you-know-who. I bent down to put it under the table leg. My head hit something hard. I knew Amy had shoved me, so I put my knee on her foot and ground it in. I quickly stood up and straightened out my apron. "Sorry about that," I said. "It's crowded down there."

Guston then set out three trays of fondue pots, one on the far end by Amy, one in the middle, and one on the near end.

"My skewer's dirty," said Amy.

"Dessert, please get this lady a new skewer," Guston said.

I tried to keep a friendly look on my face because of Guston. When I came back with the new skewer, Amy said, "Took you long enough. Were you licking the beaters in there?"

Guston's eyes were on me, so I didn't say anything back.

"Dessert," Amy continued, "what are you giving up for the Doody Drive? My sister's giving up biting her nails, and I'm giving up diet soda."

"Diet soda?" I said. "That's not even a sacrifice. Mine's way harder." (I just didn't know what it was yet.)

"It's probably baby food."

"Ha, ha," I said.

"It's cookies!" she said.

"*Way* harder," I said. (If only I knew what it was.)

"Then it has to be dessert," she said. "But I *know* you wouldn't give up dessert."

"How do you *know*?" I said.

"Because you'd never make it."

"I would so."

"Prove it," she said.

"I will," I said. "I mean—"

"EXCUSE ME, JULIE!" Amy shouted. "EXCUSE ME, EVERYBODY. I HAVE AN ANNOUNCEMENT TO MAKE. DESSERT SCHNEIDER IS GIVING UP DESSERT FOR THE DOODY DRIVE!"

CHAPTER SEVENTEEN

THE CRYSIES

And that's when the tears came. They were rolling down and I couldn't stop them. I headed straight into the kitchen and went back behind the pastry station. At least it was a little private. Amy D. had tricked me. The Leaf Stuffer had tricked me. The tears came pouring out. I couldn't stand her, and she was out there with all her sister's friends. I was alone. And now every one of them thought I was giving up dessert. There was no going back.

And then there it was. A green Jolly Rancher, over in the corner. A green Jolly

Rancher that had not been opened. Sometimes a little thing like that can keep you going. I picked it up and popped it in my mouth.

"No crying by my station!"

It was Dominique.

"Amy D.'s a witch," I said. "She tricked me."

"Chin up," said Dominique. "She must have a nice part."

"She doesn't," I said.

"It might be hidden."

"Or not there," I said.

"Sometimes it's hard to find," she said, and she held out her arms to help me up.

Then I remembered the recipe. It was sort of crumpled, but I took it out of my pocket. "Dom?" I said, as I handed it to her. "Do you think you can make these for my grandma?"

"If it's not fondue, I can make it. Let me see," she said. "Fairly basic. Chocolate, sugar, eggs . . . I can do it."

I hugged her hard.

"Now stop it," she said. "It's only a recipe."

Guston let me wash skewers and plates and pots for the rest of my "shift." I was in the sink up to my armpits and I'd been washing for a long time when I heard, "So long, Dessert!" Of course it was evil Amy. Dom was definitely wrong about everybody having a nice part, because there was no way Amy D. had one.

But a short while later, Dom appeared, with a heavenly tray of Double-Decker Chocolate Bars, the most perfect I'd ever seen, and I knew that I would do it all again, if it meant I could have a tray of these to take home.

"These things are good," she said. "Where's the recipe from?"

"It came from my Grandma Reine," I said.

"I'm putting them on the menu," she said. "What'll I call them?"

"We call them Double-Deckers," I told her.

"What was her name again?"

"Grandma Reine," I said.

"Then they'll be Grandma Reine's Double-Deckers," she said. "Yes."

"May I be the critic?" asked Guston, joining us.

"Okay," I said. Dom handed one to Guston and wrapped the rest up for me.

"*C'est divin,*" said Guston, which means it's the best-tasting thing in the world.

I didn't know how to thank Dom the right way, and I felt like I was going to cry again, so I said, "You're the best."

"Don't forget it," she said.

CHAPTER EIGHTEEN

THE BAD, THE GOOD, AND THE NEW

Around six that evening, Mummy said, "Would you please set the table?"

"Piece o' cake," I said, and I set out all the dessert plates. Then I put the Double-Ds in the middle, covered with a tea towel.

"What's under the towel?" Mummy asked.

"It's a surprise," I said. And when everybody was seated, I looked at the Beasties and I said, "This is for Grandma Reine, who went on before you were born." I looked at Charlie and said, "This is for Grandma Reine, who

went on when you were two." And then I looked at Mummy and Daddy, and I said, "This is for our Grandma Reine, who found the recipe in an overhead luggage compartment." I slowly pulled off the towel and gave each person in my family a Double-Decker Chocolate Bar, and I said, "I'm sorry."

"Your grandmother would be proud of you," said Mummy. "I know I am."

"I think she'd like Dom, too," I said, "and I have another surprise."

"Another?" said Mummy.

"There's a new dessert on the menu at Fondue," I said.

"Says who?" said Dad.

"Says Dom," I said. "The new dessert is called Grandma Reine's Double-Deckers— Dom thinks they're good." Then I looked at them both and added, "I couldn't have made it without her."

Mummy's eyes didn't just crinkle, they were really smiling. "My mother would have said it was all meant to be, Dessert—the bad, the good, and the new."

The bad, the good, and the new—they all fit together. I felt like myself again. I was forgiven.

CHAPTER NINETEEN
THE CONTRACT

At supper the next day, Mummy said, "Let's fill out that contract for the Doody Drive. I'm afraid we'll lose it if we don't take care of it. What are you going to give up?"

"Dessert," I said.

There was silence.

"I am giving up dessert," I said.

Mummy and Daddy just stared at me.

So I sang, "Heeeeeeellllloooooooooooo-ooooooooooooooooooooooooo! Is anybody hooooooooooooooommmmmmmme? I am giving up deeeeeeessssssssssssssssseeeeeeeeerrrrrrrrrrrrrrrrrrrrrrrrrrrttttttttttttttttttttttttttttt."

Mummy was white. "Did you say you're giving up dessert?"

"Yes, Mummy," I said. "I *am* giving up dessert."

"One question," said Daddy. "Why?"

"Not telling," I said.

"Couldn't you pick something reasonable?" said Dad.

"Yes, honey. It's going to be very hard for you," said Mummy. "We do have dessert every night before dinner. Did you think about that?"

"I can do it," I said.

133

"Then let's look at the contract," said Daddy.

"Hmm," he said. "This seems pretty clean. I just want to make sure you understand your commitment. No dessert for two weeks."

"Are there any other rules?" I said.

"Nope. It's all pretty clear," he said. "No troubling fine print."

"Just give up dessert, right?" I said.

"And we have to pledge you," Dad said. "Let's see. Two weeks is fourteen days. Hmm. I'll pledge you two dollars a day."

"Two?" I said. "How about three? It's not like I'm giving up mayonnaise, Dad."

"Point well taken, Dessert," said Daddy. "Three it is. Let's sign."

CONTRACT

FIRST ANNUAL DOODY DRIVE
Be a Doozie / Make a Difference
STUDENT: _Dessert Schneider_
TEACHER: _Mrs. Howdy Doody_
GRADE: ___3___

I, _Dessert Schneider_, pledge to give up _dessert._

I, _ERIC SCHNEIDER_, pledge $~~2~~ $3 per successful day.

Please add a check mark ✔ for each day you succeed!

Make checks payable to Lambert Elementary First Annual Doody Drive (upon completion).

CHAPTER TWENTY

NO DESSERT FOR DESSERT

That very next Monday was the first day of the Doody Drive. I gave my contract to Mrs. Howdy Doody.

"Dessert Schneider," she said. "You are giving up dessert? The kind that comes after a meal?"

"The kind that comes before a meal in the Schneider house. We march to our own drummer."

"Very good," said Mrs. Howdy Doody. "This is a real sacrifice for you, but I know you can do it." I knew I could do it too, especially because Daddy told me there was no fine print.

Just as Mummy had predicted, we did have dessert that night. Daddy wasn't there, because there was a roof leak at Fondue. Our table was set, but I saw only four little plates. Each one had a petit four on it. A petit four is a tiny, tiny cake, with tiny, tiny layers. It has different kinds of tasty filling between each layer and beautiful colored icing on top. A petit four looks like the most delicate and dainty gift in the world. Mushy had a tangerine-colored petit four. Wolfgang had a pink one, and Mummy and Charlie had chocolate ones. "Mummy, where is my petit four?" I asked.

"You do not have a petit four, Dessert. You gave up dessert for the Doody Drive."

"Mummy, I have pledged to make a difference, but that does not mean there should not be a petit four on my plate. There is all the more reason for me to have a petit four tonight, Mummy, so that I can give it up."

"Are you sure you want a petit four, Dessert?"

"Yes," I said.

So Mummy brought over a sky blue petit four on a little plate for me. I said, "Now I am going to give up this petit four." I walked behind the counter and opened a drawer. Just as I expected, there was the aluminum foil. I pulled off a small square and wrapped up my petit four. Then I

went to another drawer and took out a roll of masking tape, and I put a small piece on my package. I wrote, "Sky blue petit four." Then I put the little package in a grocery bag and said, "I'll be right back." I went downstairs to the freezer and placed my bag inside.

By the time I came up, they had all finished their petit fours, and I said, "Mummy, I'd be delighted to clear the petit-four plates."

"Dessert," said Mummy, "did you just wrap up your petit four and put it in the freezer?"

"Yup," I said. "Daddy said there was no fine print in my contract."

"I suppose that's true," said Mummy.

CHAPTER TWENTY-ONE

GIVING UP AND SAVING

On the second day of the Doody Drive, Mrs. Howdy Doody asked, "How many of you were able to last a whole day?" Most of us raised our hands. "Almost unanimous," she said.

"Emily V., how did it go with the gumballs?"

"Good," said Emily V.

"I can hear that platform being hammered," said Mrs. Howdy Doody. "Did you stay out of the makeup, Geezy Lou?"

"I tried to. I just got into a little lipstick."

"If at first you don't succeed," said Mrs.

Howdy Doody, "try, try again!"

"Did you do without your action figures, Donnie?"

Donnie nodded.

"How about you, Dessert?"

"I gave up my petit four last night," I said.

"Was that hard?"

"Depends how you look at it," I said.

"How do you look at it?"

"I'm thinking about it a different way," I said. "I'm not thinking about it as giving something up; I'm thinking about it as saving something."

"What do you mean?"

"I mean," I said, "that I'm giving up each dessert and saving it in the freezer. I'm saving it until the Doody Drive is over."

"Giving up and saving at the same time," she said. "Why, I never thought about that. You can give something up one moment and you can, at the same time, save it for another moment. It's a way of rewarding yourself with something you already have." Then Mrs. Howdy Doody took an Oreo out of her top right drawer, held it up, and said, "Well, well, well, what do we have here? I think I'll save this for later!"

CHAPTER TWENTY-TWO

JUST A SNACK

About a week into the drive, I was doing all
right with the sacrificing, saving all the desserts I could freeze. Then the weather turned
colder, and Mummy got out my parka. On the
way to school, I put my hand in my pocket and
found something, something small and hard.
That something was a mini Kit Kat. I didn't
remember where it came from. I decided it
would be okay to eat for two reasons: It was
officially a "snack" candy, and it was not
going to be eaten right "before" a meal like a
dessert would be. I unwrapped it.

I started to put it in my mouth when I remembered the bad, the good, and the new. I remembered the Double-Deckers and Grandma's spoiled birthday and the terrible party. I remembered how it felt to be forgiven. And I remembered how Dom said the Double-Ds were good, and how she put them on the menu (without asking Daddy). I knew then that I didn't want to make a mistake. I didn't want to eat it. I wanted to save it for later.

I put it back in my pocket, and at home that afternoon, I wrapped it in aluminum foil and put it in the freezer with a label that said, "Old mini Kit Kat."

For the second week of the Doody Drive, I kept my courage and determination, and I wrapped up whatever I could. Finally it was the last night of the drive. Mummy served fresh pineapple for dessert, so I didn't freeze it. I don't really think fresh fruit is a dessert.

Then Daddy made cheese omelets, with plenty of dipping sauce on the side.

I loved having breakfast food for supper. Daddy said, "Is this the last day of the drive?"

"Yes, it is," I said. "I can't wait until tomorrow."

"What are you going to do with all your sweets?" asked Mummy.

"I haven't decided yet," I said, but I sat tall because I *did* have a plan.

That night I lay in front of a good-smelling fire. I knew that I had made it. I caught myself smiling. Usually I hated it when I caught myself smiling, but tonight I didn't mind. After Charlie and the Beasties went to bed, Mummy said, "Are you looking forward to tomorrow?"

"Yes," I said. "I've had just about enough of this giving up and saving. Will you tuck me in?"

"Of course," said Mummy, and when she tucked me and Chunky in, she showed me a check, made out to the Lambert Elementary First Annual Doody Drive, for forty-two dollars—three dollars for each day I honored my contract.

"You made it," she said when she kissed me good night.

CHAPTER TWENTY-THREE

CLOCKWORK

I woke up at five thirty the next morning. It was time to take a look at what I'd saved. I gave Chunky a nudge, and together we practically flew down to the freezer. THE DRIVE WAS OVER! I opened the freezer and there, before my very eyes, neatly packed into a brown grocery bag, was two weeks' worth of dessert, each one labeled with masking tape and a black pen. I lugged the bag up the stairs, quiet as a mouse.

I arranged the desserts around the table, just like a clock.

I started at midnight. I put the Death by Chocolate there because anything chocolate is always my first choice. The flourless chocolate cake was at one o'clock, and the birdy nest was at two o'clock. The Snickers cake was at three o'clock, petit four at four o'clock, chocolate cupcake with vanilla icing covered with M&Ms at five o'clock, and rocky road fudge at six. Then I continued around the clock with my pineapple upside-down cake, my lumberjack, my seven-layer bar, my raspberry truffle bar, my snickerdoodle, and my apricot pocket. I was back at midnight, and I took the M&Ms off of my cupcake to make a long hand and a short hand for my clock. I joined the long hand with the short hand by putting my old mini Kit Kat in the very middle.

I took a good, long look at my wonderful, delicious clock. I remembered to take some precautionary measures while it thawed out a little. I made my bed, picked up my clothes, put on the green-flowered dress Mummy likes best (even though it's uncomfortable), combed my hair and put the matching flower clip in it, and made sure my backpack was ready. Chunky and I went back downstairs, and he stationed himself under the table, and I got a plate, I got a fork, and I sat myself down at midnight for the first taste.

I moved right around the clock.

At seven, I tried the buttery, brown-sugary pineapple upside-down cake. "This is better than the Death by Chocolate," I whispered to Chunky. "I never knew that."

I was giving him a forkful when Mummy appeared. "Chunky likes the pineapple upside-down cake," I said, hoping she'd notice that I was all ready for school. "Would you like to try some?"

"If you promise not to tell Charlie and the Beasties," Mummy said, "I'll have a taste. It's hard to resist the offer of pineapple upside-down cake first thing in the morning. But I'll bring my own fork."

She took a bite, and I said, "Mummy, how come you never told me that chocolate isn't always the best?"

Mummy shrugged. "There are some things you need to discover for yourself," she said.

And even though I was sitting in my chair, I felt like I was flying, because I didn't used to know that you could give something up and save it at the same time, and I didn't used to know that chocolate isn't always the best. I especially didn't know that sometimes dessert tastes better when you save it for last.

I never would have guessed that.

DOUBLE-DECKER CHOCOLATE BARS

2 well-beaten eggs
1 cup sugar
1 cup sifted flour
½ cup chopped pecans
About 1½ sticks butter
2 1-oz. squares unsweetened baker's chocolate
2½ cups sifted confectionary sugar
2 tbsp. milk
½ tsp. vanilla

Combine first 4 ingredients with ¼ cup melted butter and 2 sq. melted chocolate. Spread in 8" square pan. Bake in 350-degree oven for 20-25 minutes. cool. Combine con. sugar, 2 tbsp. soft butter, milk and vanilla; spread over baked layer. Chill 10 minutes. Combine remaining choc. and 1½ tsp. butter. Spread or drizzle over top. Cool 30 minutes. Cut into bars. Yield:32 bars

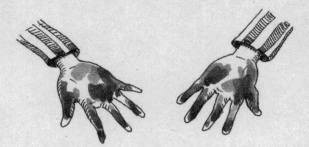

ACKNOWLEDGMENTS

To those who smoothed the way, lots and lots of love

Charlotte Steiner, because I couldn't have made it without you

Emily van Beek, my agent, for her boundless courage and determination

Bill, Christine, Kamille, Juliette, and Jacques Snell, because they are a food family, with giant hearts

Alison McGhee, for the tuck

Kate DiCamillo, for saying "Retype"

Normana Schaaf, for passion

Mrs. Hildebrand and her third-grade class at Jefferson School, 2007–2008, my helpers

Kiley Fitzsimmons, my editor, because she's unrelenting

Emma Dryden, Rubin Pfeffer, Caitlyn Dlouhy, Ann Bobco, Jeannie Ng, and Olivia Saez, for their vision

And to all those who recognize themselves on these pages!

Turn the page to find out what

Dessert

is up to next!

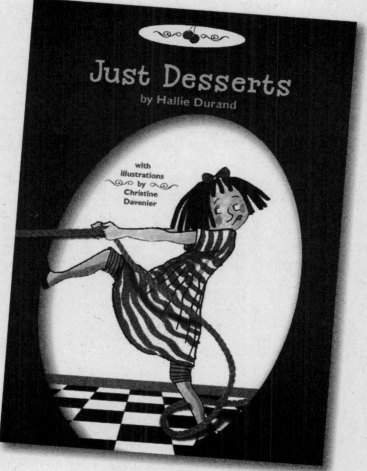

Just Desserts
by Hallie Durand

with
illustrations
by
Christine
Davenier

Available July 2010
from Atheneum Books for Young Readers

FISHING

Mummy always says that you never know what's going to happen from one moment to the next, but I think she's kookaloosa. I guess that's because every single day of my life is pretty much the same. My alarm clock buzzes at 7:10 a.m., which is just about the time Wolfie and Mushy start rattling their cribs. Wolfie is two and Mushy is one, and we call them the Beasties (that should tell you just about everything you need to know about them). After I get dressed and eat breakfast, I'm supposed to help my four-year-old sister, Charlie, get up, and it's impossible to pull her blankets down one at a time, exactly evenly, the way she likes. So she always starts screaming, and then I cover my ears, and as soon as I do, she starts clawing me. That's the bad part about Charlie. The good part about her is that she'll do whatever I want her to for a little teensy-weensy piece of gum (I store it in my jewelry box). The bus comes at 7:40, and I always let my dog Chunky out into the yard when I leave. I sit with Sharon S. and Bonnie A., behind Evan C. And when we get to school, we usually walk to Mrs. Howdy Doody's room together. She's our third-grade teacher, and I'll probably never know if that's her God-given name or not. Even lunchtime is the same every day.

Today was no different. At 11:50 Mrs. Howdy Doody said to line up, so I picked up my lunch box and I stood between Billy and Donnie. (They are twins and I've known them forever.)

Mrs. Howdy Doody opened the door, and I could smell the hot lunch in the air. I tilted my head up and sniffed to get more of the smell inside my nose. The hot lunch always smelled delicious. But then I tilted my head back down because today, just like every other day, I was not allowed to buy that hot lunch. My dad says I sound like a broken record every time I ask for it, but I think he does when he answers. He says the same thing every time:

"We're a food family, Dessert. I treat my staff like family and my family like staff." What he really means is that we own a restaurant called Fondue Paris, and he always makes some kind of meal for the staff to eat before they start working their shifts. I get the leftovers in my Thermos. And what that really means is that I don't ever get anything good for lunch.

When we got to the cafeteria, I sat down at my table with Sharon, Evan, Bonnie, Billy, Donnie, and Emily V. My lunch box smelled like 409, as usual, the same cleaning stuff my parents spray the counters with at home. It seemed just plain wrong—the hot lunch in the air smelled so good, and my lunch box smelled so bad. But I was hungry, and I didn't have anything else, so I unzipped it and opened it up. And there was that ugly metal Thermos staring up at me just like it did every other day. Crud.

I unscrewed the lid and took a look inside. I didn't like what I saw—orange-colored noodles with some little green things and clumps of mystery meat. I call it mystery meat because it's crunchy and chewy and it's not a fruit or vegetable. I stuck my fork in there and pulled out one of the crunchy-chewy clumps—for all I knew it was pigeon.

Evan saw the gook on my fork and said, "That looks like earwax."

"It's crunchier than earwax," I said. "Want to try it?"

I wasn't surprised when Evan said, "I only try things I recognize."

I twirled my fork a few times and said, "Another day, another skunk meal."

"I see why you call it that," said Emily. "It *always* smells bad."

I put my fork back in and plugged my nose with my free hand. But this time I pulled out a rind of smelly white cheese. (It looked like that rubber stuff on the bottom of my sneakers.)

I took my hand off my nose so I could touch it, and it felt like rubber too. And that's when I decided that putting my fork in that Thermos of leftover staff meal was like going fishing at the town dump. But at least it was a Friday, and I didn't have to "fish" on weekends.

The irresistible story of a boy and his wild imagination from *New York Times* bestselling author **HAVEN KIMMEL!**

"[A] hero as wild and engaging as Joey Pigza."
—*Booklist*

EBOOK EDITION ALSO AVAILABLE
From Atheneum Books for Young Readers
KIDS.SimonandSchuster.com

★ "[A] GEM OF A NOVEL."
—*Publishers Weekly*, starred review

A small town boy with a severe case of wanderlust
discovers that extraordinary things aren't just
in faraway places—they can be found right next door.

———

EBOOK EDITION ALSO AVAILABLE
From Atheneum Books for Young Readers · KIDS.SimonandSchuster.com

FRANKIE PICKLE™

REALITY IS FOR GROWN-UPS!

FRANKIE PICKLE—

A NEW CHAPTER BOOK SERIES

BY ERIC WIGHT

Published by
Simon & Schuster Books
for Young Readers

Experiment with PHINEAS L. MacGUIRE, boy-scientist extraordinaire

PHINEAS L. MACGUIRE— aka Mac—is determined to be the world's best fourth-grade scientist ever. Since he is probably the world's leading expert on mold, he has a highly scientific theory that he is already halfway there. But it is going to take some crafty— and occasionally slimy—experiments for Mac to be the best!

★"Phineas L. MacGuire proves that kids can be smart and funny."
—*Publishers Weekly*, starred review

★"Mac [is] one of the most charmingly engaging new characters in the modern chapter-book scene."—*Kirkus Reviews*, starred review